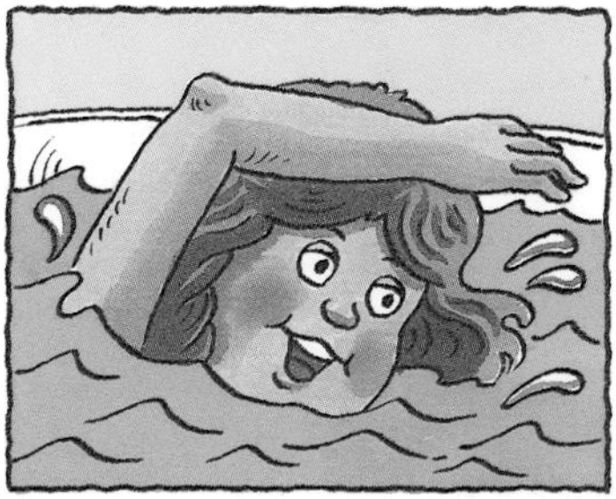

When I Play

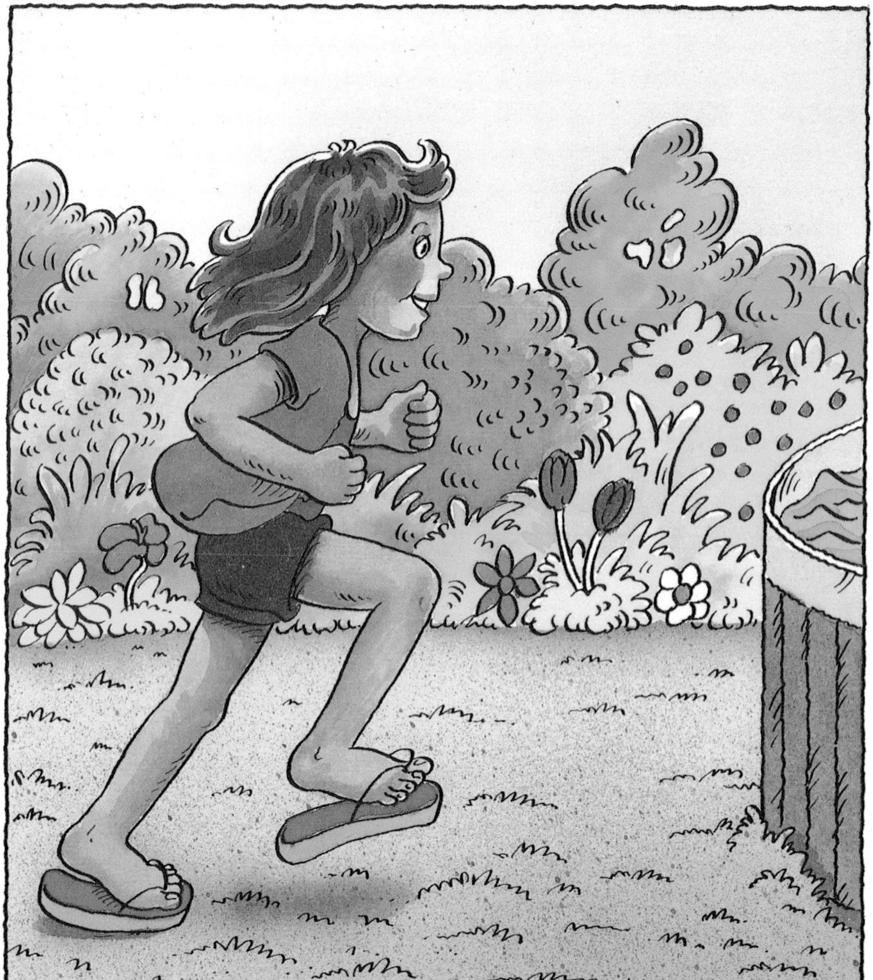

When I *r u n*, I run.

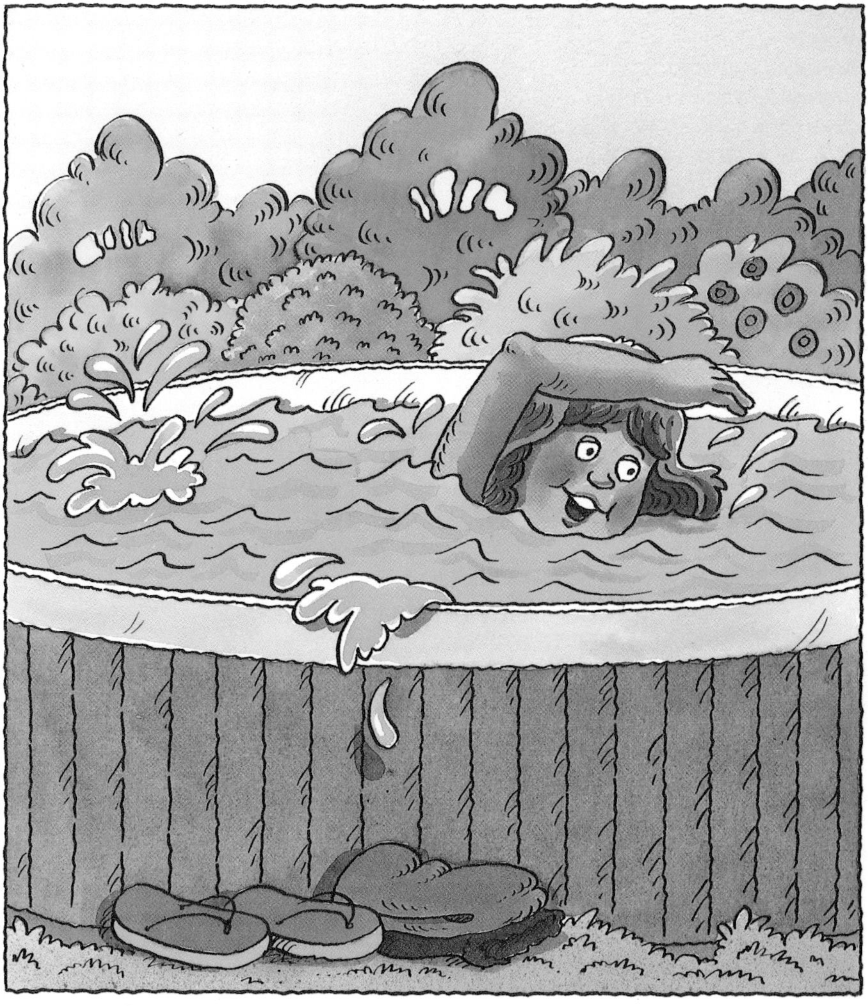

When I swim, I swim.

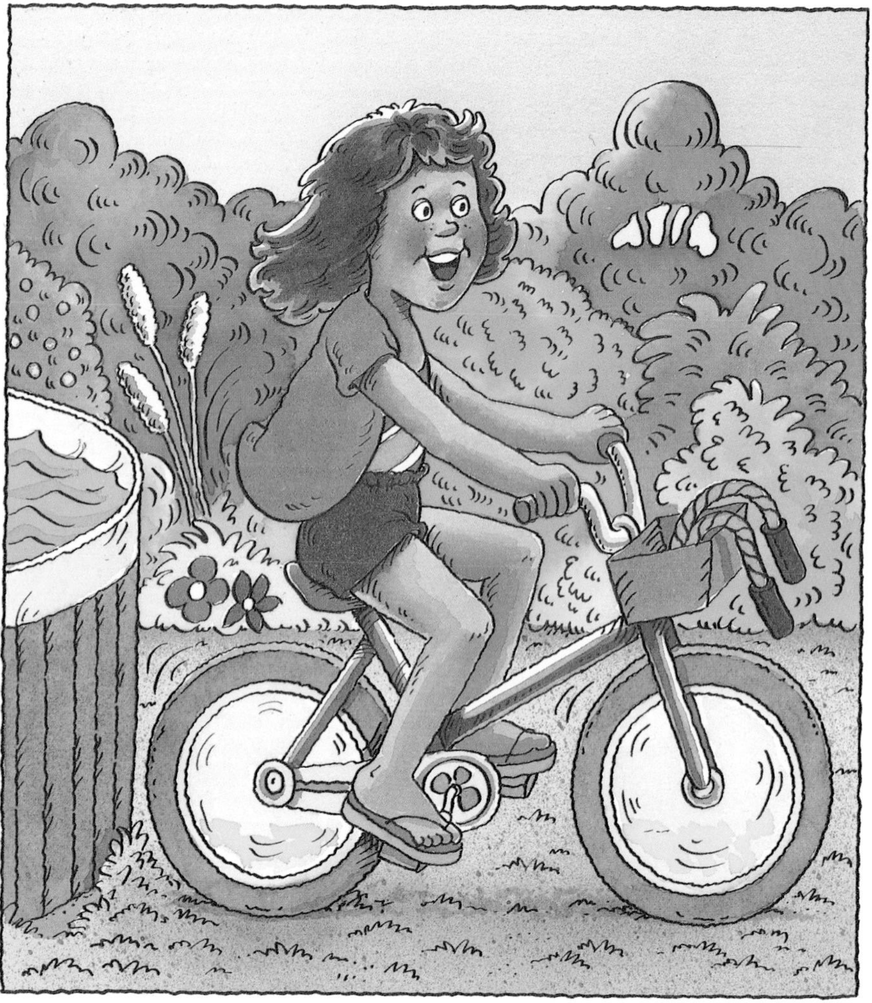

When I ride, I ride.

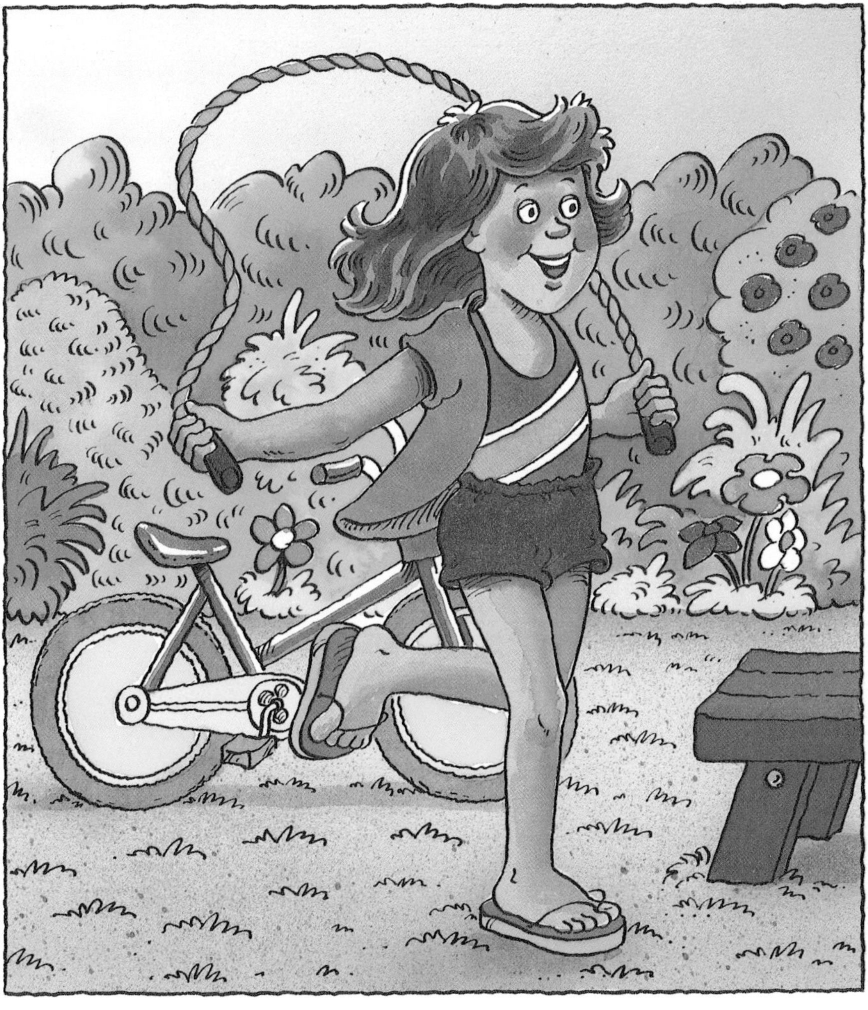

When I s k i p, I skip.

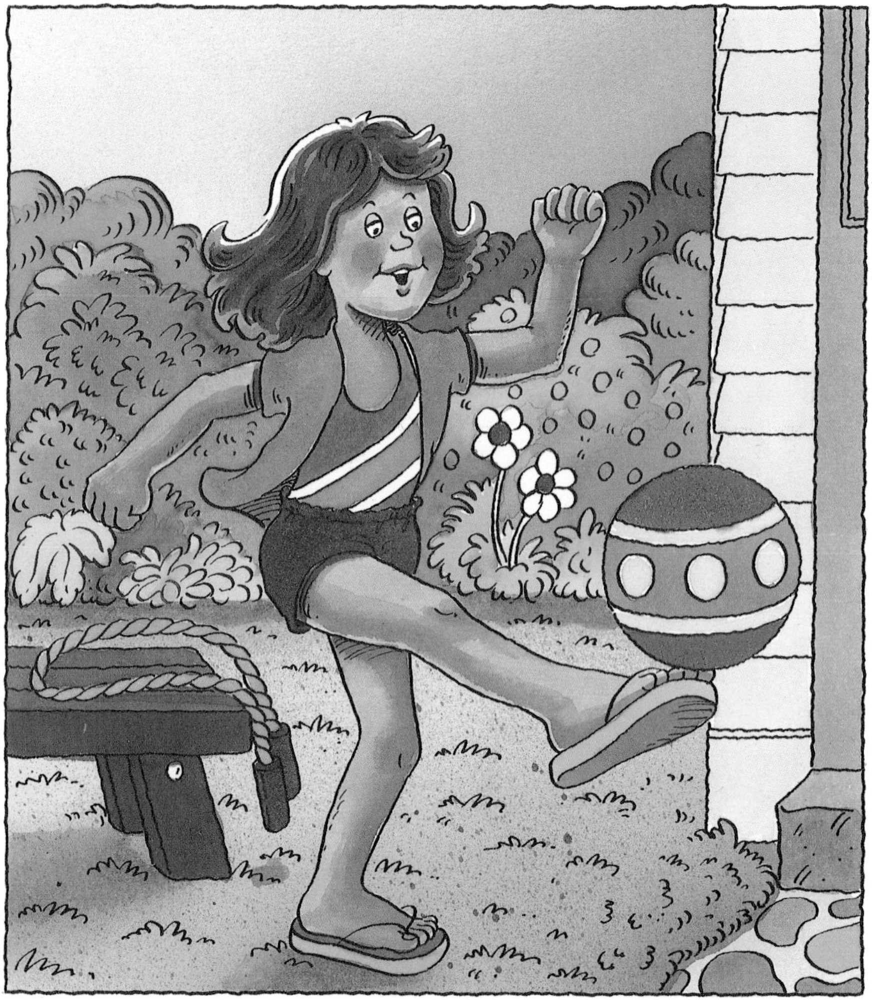

When I k i c k , I kick.

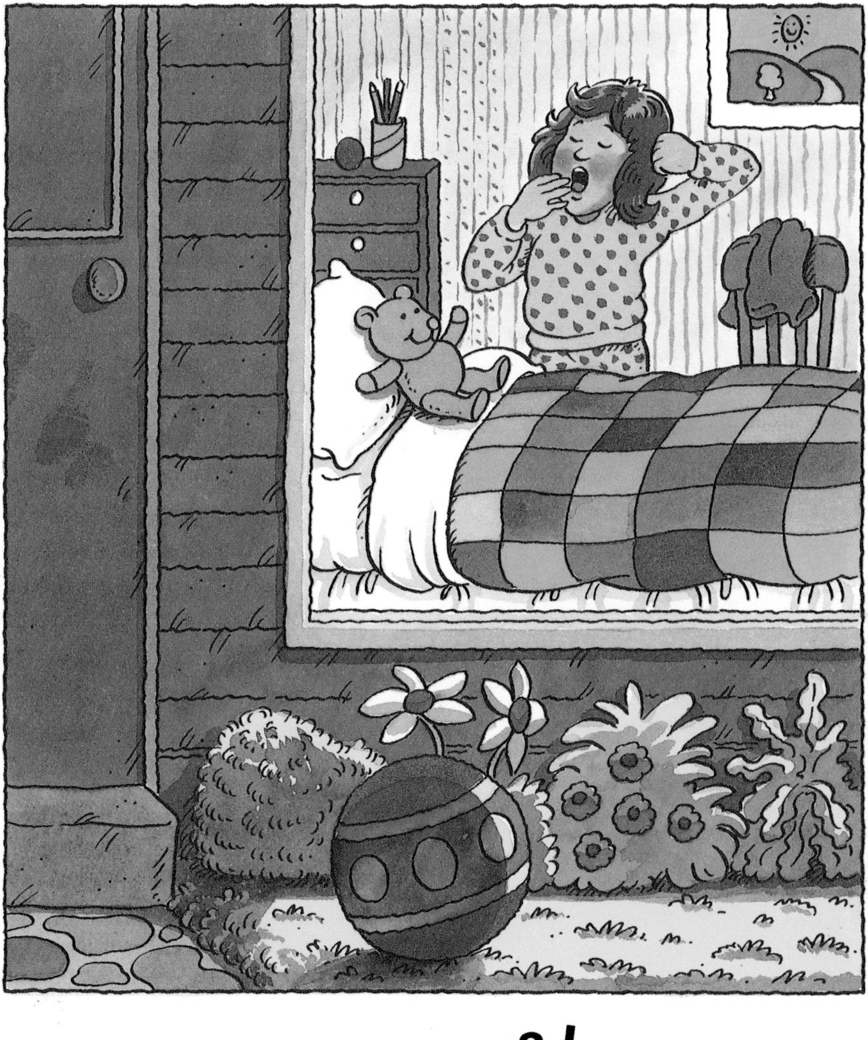

And when I sleep,

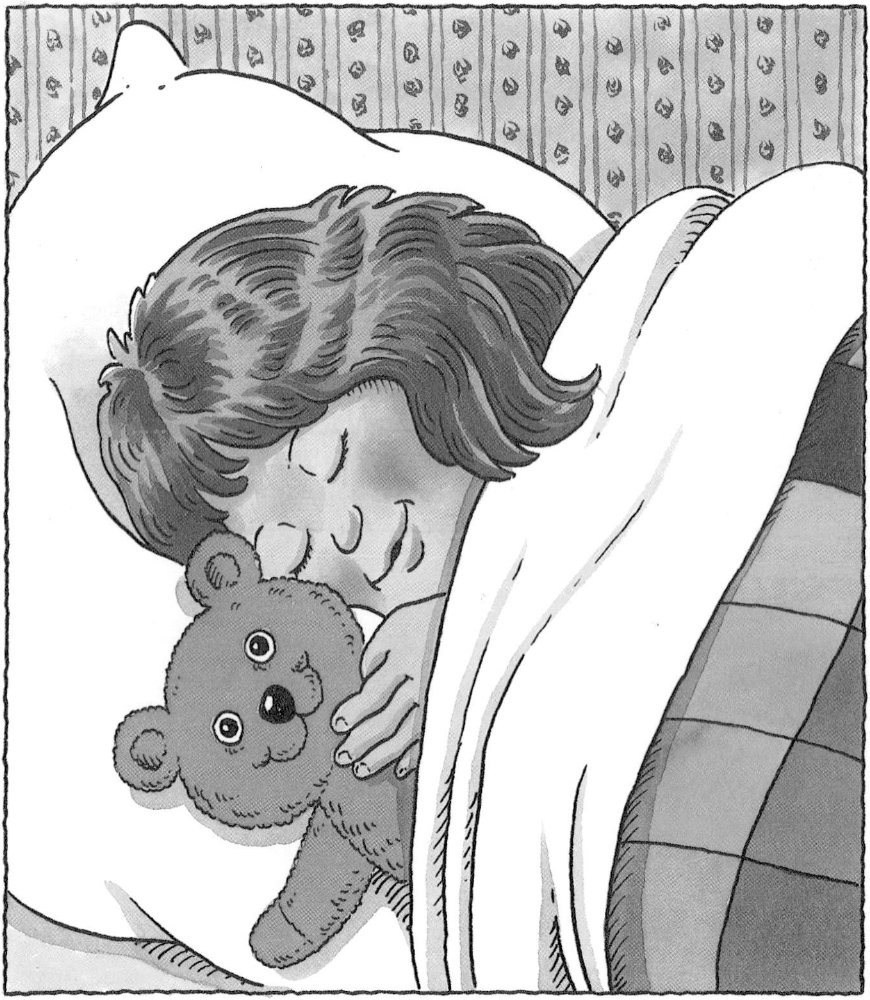

I sleep.